The BACKYARDIGANS™

Super Spies

adapted by Alison Inches
based on a teleplay written by Robert Scull
illustrated by A&J Studios

SCHOLASTIC INC.

New York Toronto London Auckland Sydney
Mexico City New Delhi Hong Kong Buenos Aires

Based on the TV series *Nick Jr. The Backyardigans*™ as seen on Nick Jr.®

ISBN-13: 978-0-545-03170-7
ISBN-10: 0-545-03170-2

12 11 10 9 8 7 6 5 4 3 2 1   8 9 10 11 12/0

Printed in the U.S.A.

First Scholastic printing, January 2008

Hello, I am AGENT SECRET.

I am a Super Spy.

I have to find **3** secret .
THREE   CONTAINERS

1 is in the .
CONTAINER ONE   CITY

2 is in the .
CONTAINER TWO   MOUNTAINS

3 is at the .
CONTAINER THREE   BEACH

is the head

MISS T.

of the spy agency.

 will give me clues

MISS T.

to help me find the .

CONTAINERS

I zoom to the  in my 🚗.
CITY   CAR

I stop at an 🍨 shop.
ICE CREAM

I order a 🍌 split.
BANANA

MISS T. appears in the BANANA split!

She gives me a clue.

Secret CONTAINER ONE 1

is in the Glass BUILDING.

I zip to the Glass 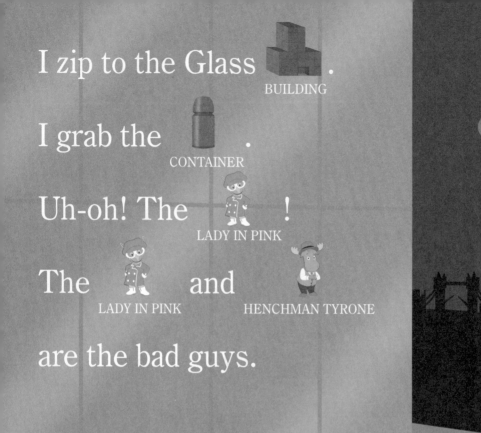.
BUILDING

I grab the [CONTAINER].

Uh-oh! The [LADY IN PINK]!

The [LADY IN PINK] and [HENCHMAN TYRONE]

are the bad guys.

No problem!

My  is also a ![helicopter] .

CAR   HELICOPTER

I get away!

I zoom to the .
MOUNTAINS

I get a .
HOT DOG

The hot dog is really a  PHONE.

 MISS T. is on the  PHONE.

She sends me to the Dairy  FARM.

At the Dairy
FARM

I grab secret  **2.**
CONTAINER TWO

Uh-oh! The  !
LADY IN PINK

No problem!

My  is also a SNOWMOBILE!

CAR

SNOWMOBILE

I get away again.

Now I zoom to the  .
BEACH

I walk into a 🧃 bar.
JUICE

I order a 🍧 .
SNOW CONE

MISS T. appears in the SNOW CONE .

She sends me to an ISLAND .

At the  ISLAND

I grab secret CONTAINER THREE 3.

Uh-oh! The LADY IN PINK again!

No problem!

My  is also a !
BOAT   JET

I jet away.

Now I have all **3** !
THREE CONTAINERS

Not so fast!

The  LADY IN PINK has  MISS T. !

The  LADY IN PINK says,

"Hand over the  CONTAINERS !"

She opens the  CONTAINERS.

She finds a GLASS,

MILK, and CHOCOLATE syrup.

The secret is CHOCOLATE MILK!

The  says

LADY IN PINK

the ▦ 🥛 is hers!

CHOCOLATE MILK

All hers!

Oops!

The  CHOCOLATE syrup is falling!

The LADY IN PINK is falling too!

"I will save you!" I say.

So I save the .

LADY IN PINK

Now the   and

want to be good guys!

A toast!

 for everyone!

Hip, hip, hooray!